Grandma
Summer

Harley Jessup

VIKING

"Slow down, Grandma!"

The car swung around a curve and Ben saw the ocean for the first time. "We're almost there, darling," Grandma said.

The car skidded onto a gravel road, and at the end of the drive Ben saw a small wooden house with shutters over all the windows. They bumped to a stop.

Ben groaned. "Is this where we're going to stay?"

"Yes, darling. Please help me get the door open."

"My name's not darling."

Together they unhooked the heavy storm door.
Grandma turned the key in the rusty lock.

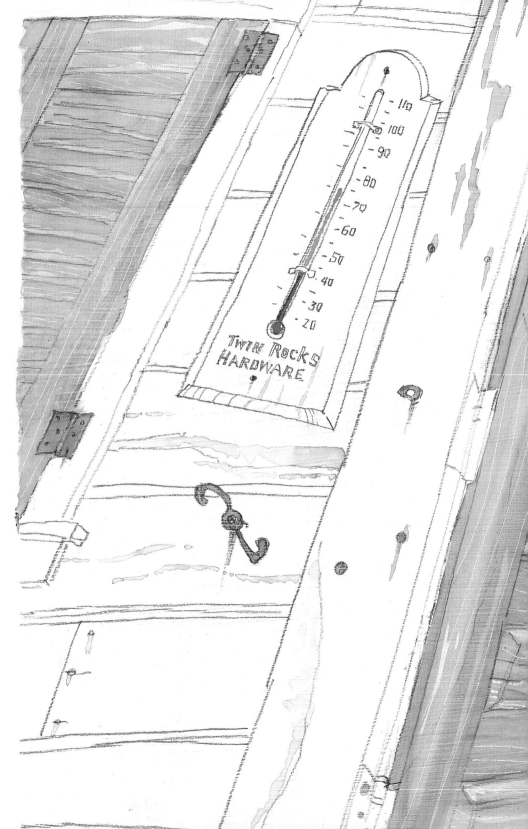

The dark house looked spooky to Ben, but
Grandma said, "Oh, I do love this old place.
It smells just like summer. Let's open up the
rest of these shutters."

After the last shutter had been opened,
Ben came in and saw his grandmother lighting a fire inside the old stove.

"That's not safe, Grandma," he warned.

She laughed. "This stove is almost a hundred years old. You have to light a
fire inside. You can cook on it, and it will heat the whole house."

"Are you almost a hundred years old, Grandma?"

"No darling, I mean Ben. Would you please bring some wood in from the garage?
We'll need to keep this fire going."

Ben went outside to the garage and pulled the big doors open.

It was spiderwebby inside and full of old stuff. Ben forgot about the wood and looked around. On a shelf in the corner he found a green glass ball.

He brought the glass ball back to show Grandma.

"What's this for?" he asked.

"My stars! Where did you find that? Here, I'll show you what it is."

Grandma drew these pictures for Ben. "It came loose from a fishing net in Japan and floated all the way across the Pacific Ocean to our beach here in Oregon."

Then she exclaimed, "The beach! We've been here all morning and we haven't been to the beach yet!"

Japanese Fishermen

GLASS FLOATS HOLD UP EDGE OF FISHING NET

They carried the picnic basket together and made their way to a huge log half buried in the sand. Grandma said, "This will do," and Ben helped her spread out the blanket.

The jelly sandwiches tasted good, and when they were gone Grandma said, "Let's put our feet in the water."

Ben stopped at the edge of the crashing waves. "No, I don't want to float across the ocean to Japan."

"Hang on!" Grandma said. Just then a big wave surged forward and swirled around them. It splashed up to Ben's knees and soaked the hem of Grandma's dress. Holding tight to each other they howled at the feeling of the cold water.

"This is fun!" Ben said.

That night, Grandma made spaghetti on the old stove and after dinner they played cards by the fire. "Do you think Japanese glass floats still wash up on the beach?" Ben asked.

"Yes, but not so many anymore," she said, looking out the window. "We'd better bring the porch chairs in. It looks like a storm's coming."

Later, as he got ready for bed, Ben could hear the rain tapping on the roof. The house creaked as the wind pushed at its walls.

Suddenly there was a loud BOOM and a flash of lightning.
The electric light went out and Ben was in the dark.

Grandma appeared at the door with an oil lamp.
"Power's out, but we'll be okay." She put the lamp down on the table,
and Ben noticed a picture of a little boy holding the green glass fishing float.

"Who's that boy?"

Grandma smiled. "That's your father when he was your age."

"Did he find the glass float?"

"Yes he did, just down at the beach where we were today." Grandma kissed Ben
good night and tucked him in under the soft quilt. He fell asleep thinking about the glass
float that had been blown such a long way across the sea.

"Wake up, darling! No time to get dressed. We've got to get down to the beach." Grandma shook Ben awake and handed him his boots.

"Why do we have to get up so early?"

"You'll see. Come on, hurry up!"

The beach had changed. They looked for the log where they had eaten their picnic, but it had been carried off by the stormy waves in the night.

The tide was out, and the sand glistened with shells, seaweed, and driftwood that had washed up in the storm.

Pointing to some people far down the beach, Grandma said, "Be quick. Those people are looking for the same thing you are."

Ben ran as fast as he could, searching every pile of seaweed and driftwood. He found clam shells, sand dollars, and a broken teacup. Under a log, he found a starfish and a little crab. There were shiny stones of every color, worn smooth by the ocean waves.

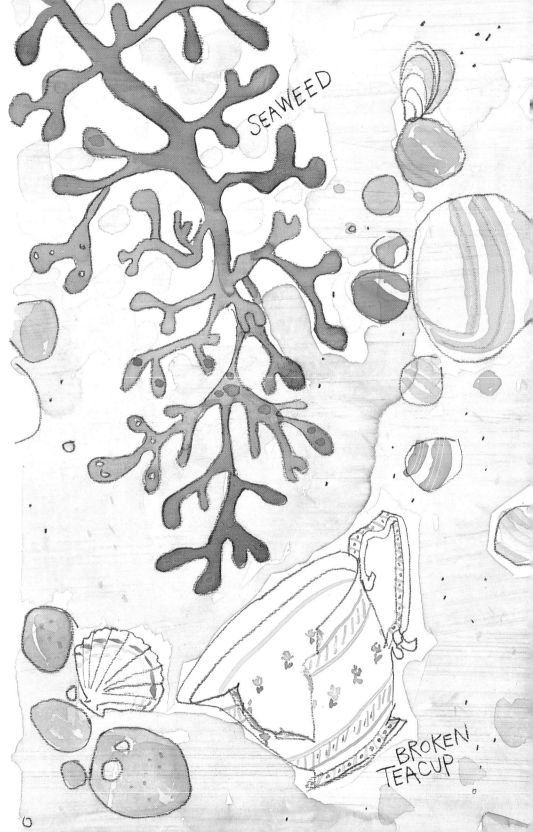

SEAWEED

BROKEN TEACUP

STARFISH

SEAWEED

AGATES

SAND DOLLAR

CLAM SHELL

MUSSEL

SCALLOP

CRAB

LIMPET

Ben was about to give up, when he saw something sparkle in a pile of driftwood. He bent closer and let out a whoop. "I found one, Grandma! I found one!"

"My stars, that's a nice big one. What a lovely green color it is!"

"Floated here all the way from Japan, right Grandma?"

"That's right, over four thousand miles. What a lucky day! Let's have some ice cream to celebrate."

"But Grandma, we haven't eaten breakfast yet."

They walked back through town with their ice cream cones. People stopped to admire the beautiful glass fishing float, and Ben told the whole story three times.

"Shall we have our picture taken?" Grandma asked.

They squeezed onto the stool in the photo booth. Ben held the glass ball up, and the camera took four pictures, one right after another.

When the photos were ready, Ben looked at them and laughed. "Grandma, I'm still wearing my pajamas!"

For my grandmother, Esther

VIKING

Published by the Penguin Group

Penguin Putnam Books for Young Readers, 345 Hudson Street, New York, New York 10014, U.S.A.

Penguin Books Ltd, 27 Wrights Lane, London W8 5TZ, England

Penguin Books Australia Ltd, Ringwood, Victoria, Australia

Penguin Books Canada Ltd, 10 Alcorn Avenue, Toronto, Ontario, Canada M4V 3B2

Penguin Books (N.Z.) Ltd, 182-190 Wairau Road, Auckland 10, New Zealand

Penguin Books Ltd, Registered Offices: Harmondsworth, Middlesex, England

First published in 1999 by Viking, a member of Penguin Putnam Books for Young Readers.

10 9 8 7 6 5 4 3 2 1

LIBRARY OF CONGRESS CATALOGING-IN-PUBLICATION DATA

Jessup, Harley.

Grandma summer / by Harley Jessup.   p.   cm.

Summary: On a visit with Grandma to the old family summer house
at the shore, Ben finds both the beach and the house filled with
history and treasures waiting to be discovered.

ISBN 0-670-88260-7

[1. Beaches—Fiction. 2. Grandmothers—Fiction.] I. Title.

PZ7.J553175Gr 1999 [E]—dc21 98-45693 CIP AC

Printed in Hong Kong

Set in Garamond Condensed